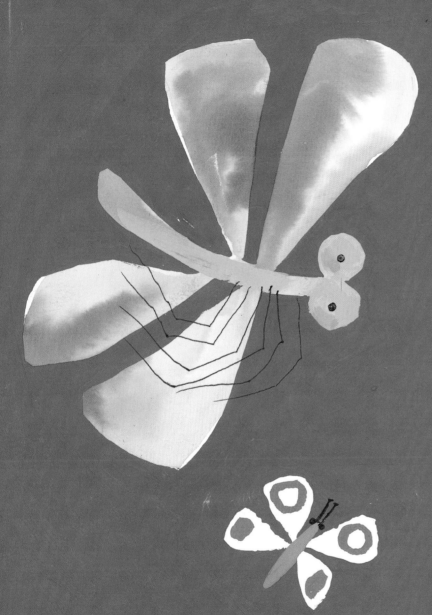

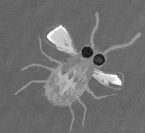

Margaret K. McElderry Books
An imprint of Simon & Schuster Children's Publishing Division
1230 Avenue of the Americas
New York, New York 10020

Text copyright © 1998 by Penelope Lively
Illustrations copyright © 1998 by Jan Ormerod
First published in 1998 by Viking, Penguin Books Ltd., London
First United States Edition, 1999

Printed in Singapore by Imago
10 9 8 7 6 5 4 3 2 1

Library of Congress Catalog Card Number: 97-76297
ISBN 0-689-82201-4

ONE · TWO · THREE

JUMP!

Penelope Lively
illustrated by Jan Ormerod

Margaret K. McElderry Books

The dragonfly had eyes that could see front,
back, and sideways.

The dragonfly could see everything at once.
She could see all of the garden.

The frog lived between two stones.
I want to be somewhere else, thought the frog.
I want to see things. I want to jump.

Let's go. One, two, three . . .

...jump!

The frog jumped as far as he could go.

"Excuse me," said a voice.
The frog looked up and saw the dragonfly.
"The garden path is not a good place for a
young frog to be," said the dragonfly.

"Why?" said the frog. "It's exciting."
"Don't ask questions," said the dragonfly.
"Just jump—quick!
One, two, three . . .

So the frog jumped . . . just in time.

The frog sat under a big leaf and looked around.
"It's good here," he said.
"There are things that wave and things
that **wobble** and mysterious shadows."

"Exactly," said the dragonfly. "That's the trouble.
Quick! One, two, three . . .

"...jump!"

The frog jumped . . . just in time.

The frog jumped out onto the lawn—
and there was the dragonfly.
"You again!" said the frog. "Now listen—
I'm as green as the grass and no one can see me.
This is where I'm going to stay."

"I wouldn't do that," said the dragonfly.
"I don't have to do what you tell me," said the frog.
"Indeed you don't," said the dragonfly.
"But if you've got any sense at all, jump!
Quick! One, two, three . . .

...jump!"

So the frog jumped . . . just in time!

He went up and up and
then he went down and down
until he dropped, *plop* . . .

. . . into the bottom of a deep hole.
"This time I'm stopping where I am,"
said the frog. "This hole will do fine.
I have a stone to get underneath if I feel like it,
and this worm to talk to if I need a friend.
And when I want to go jumping—well, I can."

"If I were you I'd jump right now,"
said the dragonfly. "Quick!"

"I'M NOT GOING TO,"
said the frog.

And then he saw what the dragonfly could see.

He jumped farther than he had ever jumped before . . .

. . . and landed with a **splash!** in the most wonderful place he could ever have imagined. "Where's this?" cried the frog.

"This is the pond," said the dragonfly.
"And it's the right place for a young frog to be.
Have fun!"

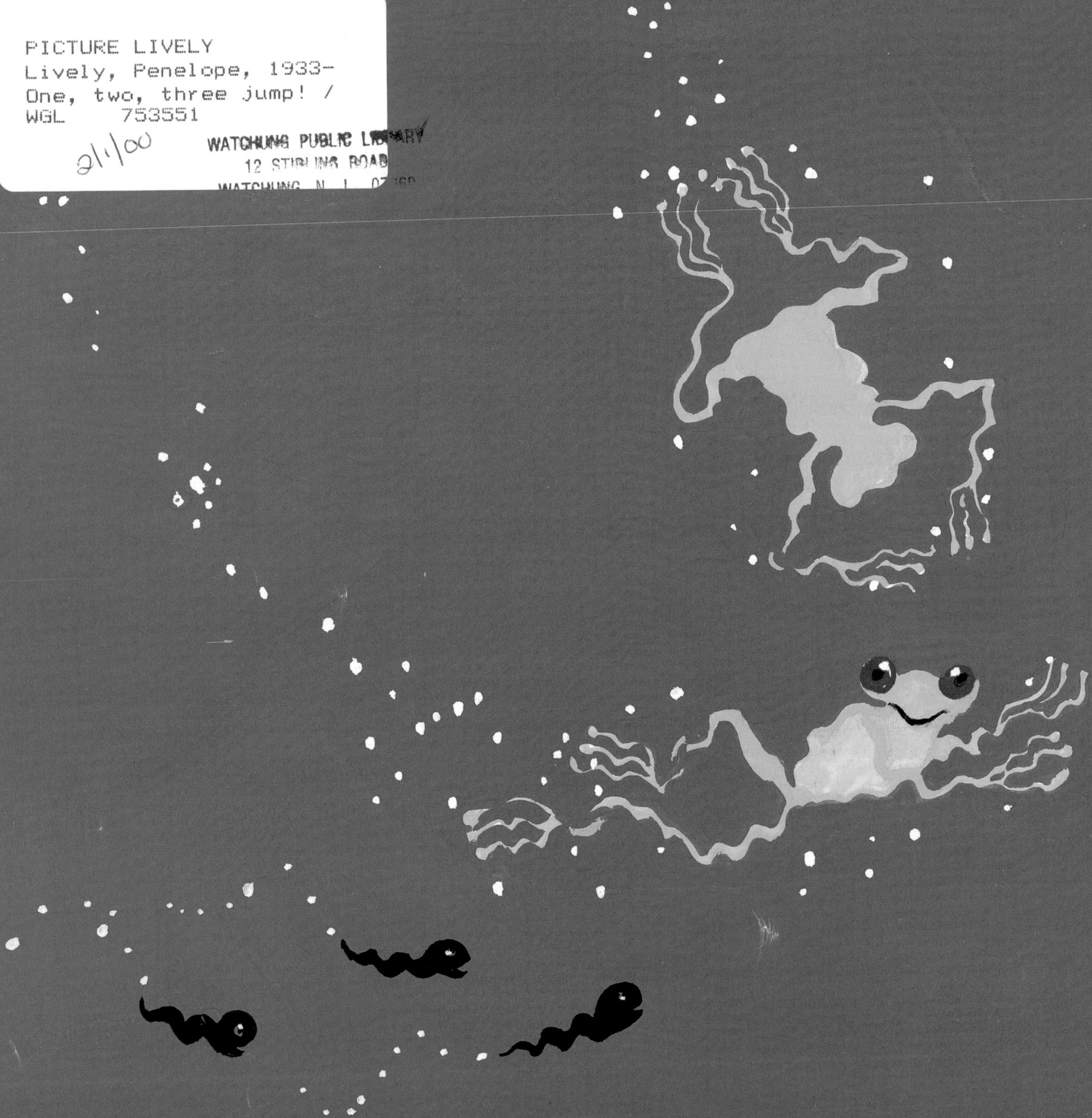